We hope you enjoy this book.
Please return or renew it by the due date.
You can renew it at

This Not Just a Book belongs to:

_____

For Klaus, danke für alles – J.W.

To Poppy and Lara – T.R.

This paperback edition first published in 2019 by Andersen Press Ltd.
First published in Great Britain in 2018 by Andersen Press Ltd., 20 Vauxhall Bridge Road, London SW1V 2SA.
Text copyright © Jeanne Willis, 2018. Illustration copyright © Tony Ross, 2018.
The rights of Jeanne Willis and Tony Ross to be identified as the author and illustrator of this
work have been asserted by them in accordance with the Copyright, Designs and Patents Act, 1988.
All rights reserved. Printed and bound in Malaysia.
1 3 5 7 9 10 8 6 4 2
British Library Cataloguing in Publication Data available.
ISBN 978 1 78344 719 0

Not Just a Book...

Jeanne Willis

Tony Ross

ANDERSEN PRESS

This is not **just** a book.

You can use it as a hat...

... or a **tent** for your **cat.**

It can keep a **table** steady.

It can prop a **floppy** teddy.

You can use it as a funnel...

... or a toy train tunnel.

A brick for building towers...

... or a thing for pressing flowers.

A book is never **just a book**.

It can swat away a fly...

... hide your face if you are shy.

Shoo away a scary bear...

... and catch a fairy in mid-air.

Or keep the **wasps** out of your **drink.**

They can make you laugh

and weep.

The End

And they can help you go to sleep.

Books can make you really clever...

... and they stay with you forever.
But the very best thing a book can do...

... is to be **read** and loved by YOU.